Robert M. De Witt

The Free and Easy Comic Songster

being a choice collection of amusing, broadly burlesque, dry, droll,

humorous and truly original songs

Robert M. De Witt

The Free and Easy Comic Songster
being a choice collection of amusing, broadly burlesque, dry, droll, humorous and truly original songs

ISBN/EAN: 9783337390228

Printed in Europe, USA, Canada, Australia, Japan

Cover: Foto ©Andreas Hilbeck / pixelio.de

More available books at **www.hansebooks.com**

FREE AND EASY

COMIC SONGSTER

BEING A CHOICE COLLECTION OF

Amusing, Broadly Burlesque, Dry, Droll,
Humorous, and
TRULY ORIGINAL SONGS.

All Adapted to very Popular Airs.

NEW-YORK :
ROBERT M. DE WITT, PUBLISHER,
NO. 13 FRANKFORT STREET.

CONTENTS.

iv CONTENTS.

FREE AND EASY

COMIC SONGSTER

I Never Mention It.

Parody on "No, We Never Mention Her."

Oh! no, I never mention it,
   The name of apple-pie ;
My lips are now forbid to taste
   The once familiar fry.
To mush and milk they hurry me,
   To ease me when I fret ;
And when they see me lift the spoon,
   They think that I forget.

They bid me seek in crackers stale
   The charm that doctors see ;
But should my strength and spirit fail,
   I'll never drink black tea.
'Tis true a year has passed, since at
   The table we were met,
I've sat me down to eat and chat,
   Yet how can I forget ?

They tell me mutton now is poor,
   The leanest of the lean ;
They hint that lambs are very thin,
   But I know what they mean.
Perhaps, like me, poor Betty Ring
   Her living may regret :
But if her appetite's like mine,
   She never can forget.

Reply to " Meet Me by Moonlight Alone."

[By Miss Pardoe.]

Meet you by moonlight ? oh ! no,
   I really can't do such a thing—
For scandal, you very well know,
   Is ever too swift on the wing.
I'm exceedingly subject to cold,
   And I cannot be looking my best,
If to you while my heart I unfold,
   I should chance have a pain in my chest.

Daylight will fully avail
   For all that you have to tell.
And so you can whisper the tale
   After luncheon,—it strikes me as well.
Oh! be sure not to ask me again,
   For though dearly your flat'ries I prize,
I am really obliged to refrain—
   They say its so bad for the eyes.

My Love She has a Red, Red Nose.

Parody on " My Love's Like a Red, Red Rose."

Oh! my love has got a red, red nose,
   I long to see it soon ;
O ! my love is like the mulberry,
   All covered o'er with bloom.

As fond as thou, my bonnie lass,
   Of full proof gin am I ;
For I will drink with thee, my dear,
   And drain the bottle dry.

I'll drain the bottle dry, my dear,
   We'll sing and dance for fun ;
And if you wish for more, my dear,
   Why, for it I will run.

But I must cut my stick, my love,
   And hop the twig ashore,
And we'll get drunk again my dear,
   A thousand times or more.

Will You trust Me then as Now.

Parody on "Will you Love Me Then as Now."

While I'm standing at the counter,
   With the ready in my fist,
As I take the I'm needing,
   On my friendship you insist;
Say you'll book me for the quarter,
   Place the chair and give the bow,
But my circumstances changing,
   Will you trust me then as now.

When my pockets once so bulging,
   Hang as loose as loose can be,
And my outward man all over
   Shows the weight of poverty;
When a change is o'er me stealing,
   Will no change you take, I vow,
Will the change find you unchanging,
   Will you trust me then as now.

Money is King.

Air :—"Things I Don't Like to See."

Oh! Money, sweet money is the theme of the play,
The poorest of beggars and rich statesmen each
      day;
By hook or by crook they look out for the vital,
Through Bulwer the author, I came by the title.
The poor parish Doctor for his service then begs,
Thus money you'll find puts us first on our legs;
Then, blest with a baby whom you love we'll sup-
      pose,
So the ready will buy it some ready made clothes.

Little boys soon grow up to manhood's estate,
Then Money's the cause of their staying out late;
A word to the ladies, for I cannot do less,
They are all for the money.   Money buys them their
    dress.
While some that have consols for their husbands
    will try,
Most ready, for ready, soon spent, then good-bye
Dear pleasures and frolics, and most things that are
    rash,
Are the means to procure and to squander the cash.

Only get change for a bill, it will soon disappear,
You'll be sure to find wants that will always seem
    clear ;
One fact is quite plain, I advise you to seek it,
If money you have then endeavor to keep it.
Some doctors will tell you, " if no cure then no pay,"
'Tis easy to promise, don't believe what they say.
The good lawyer's your friend if cash you have
    plenty,
For a debt of ten dollars they get you for twenty.

Some stupid old fathers are always for saving,
Ne'er thinking of comforts, the gold ever craving,
While many fond mothers exist uppen tea,
And ne'er think upon self for their progeny.
Now money's a good thing, and the fact will be
    found,
The road is quite easy to make happy all around.
The poor wretched gambler all honor subduing,
Would repay home and friend in plotting their ruin.

Get money if you can but abuse not its power,
'Twill give joy to your life, or embitter each hour;
Give gay parties, then soon you'll find many a friend,
Who will borrow your cash if you've any to lend;
The miser, deluded, to himself quite a pest,
Still has many warm friends who wish him at rest;
Our real wants are but few, make all happy you can,
Our bards say "a good man is a real nobleman."

If a rogue buys your vote he'll sell you in return,
For gold's the great master for it's use we sojourn;
'Twill tempt lovely women, the facts are quite cer-
    tain,
But as I've been bribed I must keep down the cur-
    tain.
This comedy, Money, will teach many a truth,
Like the " School for Scandal," give instruction to
    youth ;
When Dame Nâture and Art human natnre unfold,
Then to Bulwer and Knowles, let's repay with our
    gold.

Courting Sarah's Mother.

Air :—Umbrella Courtship.

I courted once as nice a girl,
  As any man need sigh for,
With pouting lips and teeth of pearl,
  That I went mad well-nigh for.
Her charms, in fact, entranced each sense,
  I could'nt live without her ;
For bank stock in three per cent
  Sheds golden rays about her.

Stern relatives all stubbornly
  Rejected Sarah's lover;
Yet oftentimes upon the sly
  We met, 'neath twilight's cover ;
And there within that darkened room,
  I swore by love and thunder,
That nothing save the crack of doom,
  Should rend our vows asunder.

One moonless evening fully bent
  To press my suit yet warmer,
O'er the back garden wall I went
  To seek my precious charmer ;

The casement stood ajar—within
The room I dimly spied her,
Amid the gloom like harlequin,
I bounded in beside her.

Then dropping on my knees, a rush
Of words each wish expressing,
'Tis folly beating round the bush,
When time and duns are pressing.
Pour'd from my lips " Oh, dearest maid,"
I said, " Than angel fairer !",
The boon for which so oft I prayed,
Grant me this night, sweet Sarah !"

" Your mother scolds, your father growls,
Your brother swears he'll flay me,
But I despise their threats and scowls,
Your frowns alone would slay me.
Oh, let me hear thee say I'm thine,
In whispering tones of honey ;
I only have your love divine,
(Though added, and your money.")

" Come fly with me! and never mind
The old folks cruel snarling ;
They'll soon come round when e'er they find
The knot's been tied, my darling.
Just then the door flew open wide,
And in walked pa and brother ;
When lights they bore, reveal'd that I'd
Been courting Sarah's mother.

The Sentimental Cobbler.

Air :—Derry Down.

A cobbler I am and no jobs I refuse,
I live by the mending of old boots and shoes ;
I leather my customers, stop broken holes,
And am always repairing some very bad soles.
CHORUS :—Down, Down, Derry Down.

Whenever a man's understanding is gone,
'Tis I that can mend it, tho' e'er so much worn,
Then pray good customers on me depend,
To your troubles I can very soon put an end.

'Tis not very often my work idly lacks,
For to it I stick night and morn tight as wax;
Then surely my business it never can fail,
While all sorts of jobs I continually nail.

Like all auctioneers, I'm a bit of a crammer,
Like them too I frequently work with the ham-
    mer.
Insulted one day by an ill-natured clown,
Like my auctioneer brother, I knocked him flat
    down.

Saint Monday, like others I merrily keep,
And few are the sorrows that make me weep;
I forget all disasters, forgive all that's past,
And swear all the day to be true to the last.

My hair often bristles to think all my life,
I have lived without taking a lass for my wife;
But as I'm grown old and no chance can well fall,
I'll wait for grim death, and then give up my *awl*.

The Perfect Cure.

[An Original Version]

Young love he plays some funny tricks
    With us unlucky elves;
So gentlemen I pray lookout,
    And take care of yourselves;
For once I met a nice young maid,
    Looking so demure,

And all at once to me she cried,
 "You are a perfect cure."

I wasted on her lots of cash,
 In hopes her love to share,
I used with her to cut a dash,
 And all things went on square;
Until I caught another chap
 Who on his knees did woo her,
She cried as he my face did slap,
 "You are a perfect cure."

I called upon her the next day,
 Concerning that affair?
I took a seat, and on it lay
 A strange hat, I declare.
" Whose hat is that," says I; says she
 " Not yours, you may be sure,
So you may walk your chalks from me,
 For you are a perfect cure."

" You are no cure," I replied;
 " Such insults are not needed,"
When a tall fellow I espied
 Who nearly half killed me, did;
I through the window took a leap,
 And fell into the sewer;
They dragged me out and loud did shout,
 " You are a perfect cure."

I was laid up ill for seven months,
 Indeed I'm not romancing,
Which brought on old Tantany's dance
 And then I kept on dancing.
One day a peeler called on me,
 I felt ashamed you'r sure,
" Along with me, come on," says he,
 " You are a perfect cure."

He took me to the magistrate,
    And there stood faithless she,
An artful tale she did relate,
    And then swore against me.
The case created lots of fun
    At my expense to be sure,
So I pay for what I never done
    Aint I a perfect cure.

A cure the neighbors now call me,
    My friends all say the same,
They try to cure me of my love,
    And rob me of my name.
I've told you all, my song is done,
    You'll pity me I'm sure,
And say, as I away does run,
    There goes the perfect cure.

I Stood on the Shore.

As sung by E. T. Thorne.

I stood on the shore 'midst the weeping and wailing,
    Of friends that were parting it might be forever;
They gave a loud cheer when the good ship was
        sailing,
    And wept while the echoes were dying away.
One bright face was laughing while tears chased
        each other,
    It was but an infant whose smile I saw there ;
The babe had its home on the breast of its mother,
    But little it knew of its mother's despair.

That morn to the wars went, the husband and father,
    The tears of the mother fell fast on the child ;
I wept, for the drops in my own eyes would gather,
    I spoke and the infant looked upward and smiled ;
I talked of old homes and the deeds of proud story,
    The wife thought of battles that still were to
        come ;

I said in my mind, they who fight for our glory,
  Shall never have fear for the loved ones at home.

And spoke I not the truth, where's the freeman who
    falters,
  To bear out the promise a nation has made?
If dear to our hearts are our homes and our altars,
  Then those that defend them shall loose not our
    aid.
Humanity needs it, her pealings are holy,
  And justice demands that each man plays his part,
We may not all fight, but the high and the lowly,
  Like freemen can aid the cause we have at heart.

The Tea! The Tea!

Parody on "The Sea! The Sea!"

The tea! the tea! the toast and tea!
The black, the green, the four and three!
Without the milk, with all its grounds,
It filleth my heart with joyous bounds.
This praises ale aloud—that Mocha tries—
Or for a deep drop of the creature sighs.
I'm one for tea! I'm one for tea!
I am a stunner for bohea!
With the brew I love, with the brew of sloe,
Without all liquid else I'll go.
Tho' the milk don't come, or the sugar sweet,
What matter? 1 can drink it neat!

The cloth was white, the tea was drawn
At the breakfast hour when I was born;
The kettle whistled, so gossips told,
And the tea-pot was as full as it could hold;
And never was known such a cup of tea,
As welcomed to life the babe, (that's me.)
I have lived since then on the best Souchong
Well, just exactly my whole life long,
With wealth to spend and a power to range,
But never have thought or tried to change;
For I'm death—no matter what sort it be—
On China, or " or any other man's" tea!

Charlotte My Darling.

Parody on " Kathleen Mavourneen."

Charlotte my darling, the dinner is waiting,
The voice of the waiter is heard on the stair ;
The guests on their bosoms their napkins are pin-
ning,
Charlotte, my darling! why lingering there?
Oh, hast thou forgotten how early was breakfast?
Or hast thou forgotten how late shall be tea?
We may be too late, and we shall not get any,
Charlotte, my darling! have pity on me.

Charlotte, my darling come down from your toilet,
The fair capon's gleam in the jelly's mild light ;
Oh where is the spell that once lay in plum-pudding?
Come down as you are, or I shan't get a bite.
Charlotte, my Charlotte! my faint voice is calling,
Ere long will be vanished both pudding and tart ;
I shall be too late, and they wont give me any,
O, why dost thou loiter when they must depart?

Take Care of Your Head in the Morning.

Air :—" Over the Water with Charley."

What a pity it is that a man while he's out,
    Can't take a small drop, and rest quiet ;
Not swig till he doesn't know what he's about,
    And reel home without making a riot ;
My grandfather, Bottlenose, often would say,
    (And his caution I took as a warning,)
" My boy, if your out to-night soaking your clay,
    Take care of your head in the morning."

My old friend Tom Tipple could drink like a horse,
    And we lived in the same house to-gether,

One word with each other we never had cross,
  But were thick as young birds of a feather,
Now Tom's was a failing—a sad one, 'tis clear,
  He'd swig till the daylight was dawning,
Tho' I never ceased whispering into his ear,
  "Take care of your head in the morning."

To a party one night he was going out to sup,
  When his wife kissed his cheek rather fawning,
"At six, my dear Tommy, you'll have to get up,
  So take care of your head in the morning;"
He vow'd that no liquor should tempt him on earth
  After one glass, the rest he'd be scorning;
"I'll be home soon," said he, "dear, and snug in
    my bed,
Because of my head in the morning."

Away to the party he went very spruce,
  Of his head in the morning was thinking,
But glass after glass of the dear luscious juice,
  He pour'd down in his throttle like winking!
He took some old rum, then brandy and gin
  (For he'd not forgot his wife's warning,)
"I'm not going to mix it," says he with a grin,
  "'Cause it muddles one's head in the morning."

Then he pick'd up his legs, and towards home he
    did stump,
  Took the gas for a rushlight or candle,
Attempted to light his cigar at a pump,
  And friendly shook hands with the handle!
Swore the lamp-posts were dancing an Irish qua-
    drille,
  When a straw tripp'd him up without warning;
Bang into the gutter he roll'd—"what a gill,"
He exclaimed, "I shall look in the morning.

With the curb-stone for a pillow, contented he lay,
  Singing songs till daylight was dawning,
Says he "won't my wife be delighted, I say?

I've took care of my head in the morning !"
Then into a plug-hole he popp'd his latch-key,
   And kept twisting it, cursing and yawning;
" My fool of a wife's lock'd the street door," says
       he,
Quite forgetting my head in the morning."

The police coming by dragged him out of the mire,
   While he left and right began podging,
On a shutter they laid him against his desire,
   And found him a soberly lodging.
For assaulting the peelers and getting drunk too,
   He was fined ten bob, as a warning;
"Next time," says his honor, " I'd just advise you,
   To take care of your head in the morning."

Now friends, young and old, pray don't slight my
      advice,
   (I wish it well known in each quarter,)
Whenever your taking your grog snug and nice,
   Always mix it with plenty of water ;
Or if you prefer a drop neat, which you might,
   More than one thimble full pray be scorning,
For if you dive deep in the glass of a night,
   You'll find your head swim in the morning!

Disertation upon Noses.

[An old fashioned Comic Song.]

I forget what Sterne says in his chapter on noses,
   With laughter to make our sides ache :
But I think like Lavater he arguing supposes
   Good or ill from their shapes or their make ;
But I'll let both alone with each skit or reflection,
   As they spar or together agree,
And explain the effects in my own recollection,
   These same noses have had upon me.

Cocked up noses are pert, and some say not too civil
   Some have none, like a bear when a cub,
A fine stately nose may sometimes hide a devil,
   And an angel may beam in a snub.
The flat nose, like a platter, is scarcely worth nam-
       ing,
   The sharp nose is a pretty good sort;
The mulberry nose that like Randolph's is flaming,
   Makes one think of good claret or port.

Your fine Grecian nose, about which they so teaze us,
   Is admired, but from this some will swerve ;
For a nose should be beautiful if it would please us,
   And the true line of beauty's a curve.
The old Roman hook'd noses were guards to their
       peepers,
   They, therefore, were men of renown ;
For the sickle-like noses, armed them all so like
       reapers,
   They cut all their enemies down.

After all a good nose is a generous feature,
   To the face gives an elegant air ;
It lends grace to men, is the type of good nature,
   And is not much disliked by the fair.
But the mind is the thing for though noses be
       hooked,
   Pale, ruby, depressed or elate,
As a razor's as sharp, as a bill hook as crooked,
   Never mind, so the heart be but straight.

Dublin Sights.

Air :—Limerick Races.

When at home with dad, I never had no fun, sirs;
Which made me so mad, I swore away I'd run, sirs.
I packed up my clothes so smart, ribb'd stockings,
      vest so pretty,
With money and a light heart, tript off for Dub-
   lin City.
            CHORUS.—Tu ral, Ju ral, la.

As soon as I got there about the streets I ran, sirs,
At all the shows to stare, my rambling I began, sirs ;
O such charming sights ! Music grinding women,
Water lifting lights, crocodiles and yeomen.

> Tu ral, lu &c.

The next sight I did see, was wonderful, good lack,
  sirs,
A coach drawn by a flea, and two men made of
  wax, sirs ;
There were Kings and Queens, and lawyers without lungs, sirs,
Circassians, Gulotines, and women without tongues,
  sirs.

> Tu ral, lu, &c.

But the greatest fight I saw, from the beginning,
Was a real sham fight upon a field of linen ;
I next saw fighting cocks, but what I thought most
  rare, sirs,
Was, that up in a box, the Curragh of Kildare, sirs,

> Tu ral, lu, &c.

I to the mall was led, where I my eyes did feast, sirs,
To see a man in red exhibit the wild beasts, sirs ;
Says he, "pay and go in, I've apes and monkeys
  plenty,"
Says I, 'for one within, without I'll show you twen-
  ty."

> Tu ral, lu, &c.

To the Play-house then I goes where I saw merry
  faces,
And in the lower rows were servants keeping
  places;
'Mongst actors I found soon, they manage things
  quite funny,
For they play the Honeymoon before the farce of
  Matrimony.

> Tu ral, lu, &c.

Young Grimes.

Parody on " Old Grimes."

Old Grimes is dead that good old man,
  We ne'er shall see him more ;
But he has left a son who bears—
  The name that old Grimes bore.

He wears a coat of latest cut,
  His hat is new and gay ;
He cannot bear to view distress,
  So turns from it away.

His pants are new, fitting snug
  O'er patent leather shoes ;
His hair is by a barber curled,
  He smokes cigars and chews.

A chain of massive gold is borne
  Above his flashy vest ;
His clothes are better every day,
  Than were old Grimes's best.

In fashion's court he constant walks,
  Where he delight doth shed,
His hands are very white and soft,
  But softer is his head.

He's six feet tall, no post more straight,
  His teeth are pearly white,
His habits though are sometimes loose,
  And sometimes very tight.

His manners are of sweetest grace,
  His voice of softest tone ;
His diamond pin's the very one
  That old Grimes used to own.

A dickey tall adorns his face,
  His neck a scarf of blue ;
Sometimes he goes to church for change,
  And sleeps in old Grimes' pew.

He has drank wines of every kind,
  And liquors cold and hot ;
Johnny Grimes in short, is just the sort
  Of man, Old Grimes was not.

Der Duychman's Serenade.

Parody on " The Cavalier."

'Twas a good summer's night and der moon shone
    bright,
  Unt I felt so sholly and gay,
Ven I dout I vould go, un mine avvections to show,
  To a laty some musicks I'd blay ;
So I duned up mine vlute, and away I did poot
  To her house vere mine love she hangs out ;
Un der air it did ring mit der zongs I did zing,
  For at least half a mile round apout.
Round apout, Round apout,
  For at least half a mile round apout.

" It'll be a rich dreat to hear musick zo zweet,"
  Dus I said to menzelf as I blayed ;
" I'll enchant her by tam, zuch a tear leetle lamb,
  I ne'er saw since der tay I vas made."
Put a sash here raised, un I velt amazed,
  Ash a head from her vinder dere bops,
Un on dop ov mine crown, mit a splash dumbling
    down,
  Came a pucket of vater and schlops.
Un schlops, un schlops,
  Came a pucket of vater and schlops.

A Warning to Travelers.

Air :—" Bob and Joan."

Never go to France,
    Unless you know the lingo,
If you do, like me,
    You will repent, by jingo!
Staring like a fool,
    And silent as a mummy,
There I stood, alone,
    A nation with a dummy!
            CHORUS :—Never go, &o.

Chaises stand for chairs,
    They christen letters, " billies ;"
They call their mothers " mares,"
    And their daughters "fillies."
Strange it was to hear,
    I'll tell you what's a good 'un,
They call their leather " queer,"
    And half their shoes are wooden.
               Never go, &c

Signs I had to make,
    For every little notion,
Limbs all going like
    A telegraph in motion ;
For wine I reeled about,
    To show my meaning fully,
And made a pair of horns
    To ask for " beef and bully."
               Never go, &o.

"Moo!" I cried for milk,
    I got my sweet things snugger,
When I kiss'd Jeanette,
    'Twas understood for sugar.
If I wanted bread,

My jaws I set a going,
And asked for new laid eggs
By clapping hands and crowing.
>> Never go, &c.

If I wished a ride,
I'll tell you how I got it;
On my stick astride
I made believe to trot it;
Then their cash was strange,
It bored me every minute,
Now here's a "hog" to change,
How many "sows" are in it?

The Irish Potatoe.
Parody on the "Old Oaken Bucket."

How sweet to the taste is the Irish potatoe,
As memory awakens the thought of the plant!
Its dark verdant vine-top, and beautiful blossom,
In pleasant transition my memory haunt;
Ay, thought of the root in profusion once growing,
On the broad sunny hill-slope adjoining the mill,
At the homestead how many we raised there's no
knowing,
For some were but small ones and few in a hill.

CHORUS.

The mealy potatoe, the Irish potatoe,
The thin-skinned potatoe that grew on the hill.

That delectable plant I will prize while I'm able,
For, often at noon when returned from the field,
I found it superior to all on the table—
The best flavoured edible that nature could yield.
With what eager appetite, sharpened by labor,
I plied knife and fork with a hearty good will!
Alas! there are none of the old fashioned flavour,
None like the "real simons" that grow on the hill.

The mealy potatoe, the Irish potatoe,
The thin-skinned potatoe that grew on the hill.

How prime from the full heapen dish to receive it,
  As, poised on my fork, it ascends to my mouth!
No appeal to the palate could tempt me to leave it;
  Though affected by rot on a long summer's drouth,
And now far removed from that situation,
  Where I used to partake of the root to my fill,
Fancy fain would revert to my father's plantation,
  And sigh for the " kidney" that grew on the hill.

    The mealy potatoe, the Irish potatoe,
    The thin skinned potatoe that grew on the hill.

The Charity Boy.

(As sung by the celebrated Sam Cowell.)
Air:—."Off She Goes."

No doubt you wonder who I is,
And at my figure you may quiz;
At once your doubts then to destroy,
I'm Bobby Miles, the Charity Boy.
Tho' some folks say as I'm a fool,
I'm a teacher in a Charity School;
And 'cause I am six feet to view,
I'm reckon'd the head scholar too.

CHORUS.

O, what a pleasure learning is!
For tho' the folks may jeer and quiz,
I'm mammy's pet, and daddys's joy,
O, what do you think of the Charity Boy?

My talent I did quickly show,
At twelve years old, why you must know,
Pot-hooks and hanger, I wrote free;
Beside, I know my A. B. C.
My rising genius not to pass,
They promoted me to the fust class.
And ven the teacher the boys did whack,
I'd the honor to take them on my back.

    O, what a pleasure, &c.

I'm so accomplished, you may see,
At marbles none can play like me,
At buttons, too, I comes it stout,
I beats my playmates out and out.
At larning, too, no one denies,
And this ere proof will quite suffice ;
You hear as I can spell quite pat,
C A T dog, and D O G cat.

       Oh, what a pleasure, &c.

Von afternoon I play'd the vag,
And to the fields my way did drag,
To get cock-sorrel ; the place I know,
And butter-cups and daises too.
Next day the teacher scolded me,
And threatened that I horsed should be ;
But when he made the fust attack,
Why, I wollop'd him just like a sack.

       Oh, what a pleasure, &c.

So this you see how blest I are :—
In larning I bang's Byron far.
With a mind content wher'er I goes,
And dress'd in these ere handsome close,
I never bless the fate, I'm sure,
Which made me humble—made me poor ;
For, oh! you can't conceive the joy
It is to be a Charity Boy.

    Humpy dumpy on the wall,
    Humpy dumpy got a fall ;
    I'm mammy's pet and daddy's joy,
    So, wot d'ye think of the Charity Boy.

No Irish Need Apply.

[Original version by F. B. Philips.]

Sure, I was out the other night, on such a wild-
     goose chase,
I saw an advertisement about a dacent place ;

It is myself it would well suit, but I cannot tell
          you why,
The man he said, " did you not read ' no Irish need
          apply.'"
                    CHORUS.
If 'tis my country you dislike, I'm sure I don't
          know why,
Faith it's all blarney when you say, "No Irish
          need Apply."

Just take a trip to Ireland they will treat you like
          a man,
The whiskey they'll pour into you as long as you
          can stand;
With heart and hand they'll welcome you, tell me
          the reason why,
Our ears offend with that dainty end, ".No Irish
          need apply."
So just look out, and mind yourself, for I say by
          the by,
You lose your senses when you say, " No Irish
          need Apply."

You talk about your soldiers, now tell me if you
          can,
If the bravest of them all are not Irish men;
In America, in China, and India bye the bye,
You never say when you want men, "No Irish
          need Apply."
You may talk about your country, but you know
          'tis all my eye,
For the best feather in your cap, is when " Irish do
          apply."

Of Generals and Statesmen, old Ireland can boast,
Her Poets, too, 'tis well known to you, are univer-
          sal toasts;

There's Goldsmith, Moore and Lover, and Morgan
 bye the bye,
You could not get their equals if "No Irish need
 Apply."
So to conclude, toss off your glass, I see no reason
 why,
You should put in your advertisement "No Irish
 need Apply."

Love and Physic.

Air :—" Bow Wow."

A clever man was Doctor Digg,
 Misfortunes well he bore, sirs,
He never lost his patience, till
 He had no patients more, sirs;
And though his practice once was large,
 It did not swell his gains, sirs,
The pains he labored for, were but
 The labor for his pain, sirs.

> That's just so,
> Tol lol de riddle lol,
> And that's just so.

To marry seemed the only way
 To ease his mind of trouble,
Misfortunes never singly come,
 And misery makes them double.
He had a patient rich and fair,
 That hearts by scores was breaking;
And, as he once had felt her wrist,
 He thought her hand of taking.

> That's just so, &c.

And so he called ; his aching heart
 With anxious fear was swelling,

He, half in habit took her hand,
   And on her tongue was dwelling.
But thrice, though he essayed to speak,
   He stopped, and stuck, and blundered,
For say, what mortal could be cool,
   Whose pulse was most a hundred ?
                 That's just so, &c.

" Madame," at last he faltered out,
   His love had grown courageous—
" I have discerned a new complaint.
   I hope will prove contagious ;
And when the symptoms I relate,
   And show its diagnosis,
Oh, let me hope from those dear lips,
   Some favorable prognosis !"
                 That's just so, &e.

" This done," he cries, " let's try those ties
   Which none but death can sever ;
Since ' like cures like' I do infer,
   That love cures love forever."
He paused—she blushed—however strange
   It seemed on first perusal,
Although there was no promise made,
   She gave him a refusal.
                 That's just so, &c.

Perhaps you think, 'twixt love and rage,
   He took some deadly potion,
Or with his lancet oped a vein,
   To ease his pulse's motion.
To guess the vent of his despair,
   The wisest one might miss it,
He reached his office,—then and there—
   He charged her for the visit.
                 That's just so, &c.

The Old Bachelor.

(A Popular Comic Song.)

When I was a school boy, aged ten,
  Oh mighty little Greek I knew ;
With my short striped trousers, and now and then,
  With stripes on my jacket, too!
When I saw other boys to the playground run,
  I threw my old gradus by,
And left the task I had scarcely begun,
  " There'll be time enough for that said I."

I was just nineteen when I fell in love,
  And I scribbled a deal of rhyme.
And I talked to myself in a shady grove,
  And I thought I was quite sublime.
I was torn from my love—'twas a dreadful blow!
  And the lady, she wiped her eye,
But I didn't die of grief—oh, dear me, no!
  " There'll be time enough for that," said I.

My next penchant was for one whose face
  Was her fortune—she was fair ;
Oh, she spoke with an air of enchanting grace,—
  But a man cannot live upon air.
And when poverty enters the door, young love
  Will out the casement fly ;
The truth of the proverb I'd no wish to prove,
  " There'll be time enough for that," said I.

My next was a lady who loved romance,
  And wrote very splendid things,
And she said with a sneer, when I asked her to dance,
  " Sir, I ride upon a horse with wings."
There was ink on her thumb when I kissed her hand,
  And she whispered, " If you should die,
I will write you an epitaph, gloomy and grand."
  " There'll be time enough for that," said I.

I left her, and sported my figure and face
 At opera, party and ball;
I met pretty girls at every place,
 But I found a defect in them all.
The first did not suit me, I cannot tell how,
 The second I cannot say why;
The third—bless me, I will not marry now,
 "There'll be time enough for that," said I.

I looked in the glass, and I thought I could trace
 A sort of a wrinkle or two,
So I made up my mind that I'd make up my face,
 And come out as good as new.
To my hair I imparted a little more jet,
 And I scarce could suppress a sigh,
But I cannot be quite an old bachelor yet,—
 "No, there's time enough for that," said I.

I was now fifty-one, yet I still did adopt
 All the airs of a juvenile beau;
But somehow, whenever a question I popp'd,
 The girls, with a laugh, said "Oh no!"
I am sixty to day, not a very young man,
 And a bachelor doom'd to die,
So youths, be advised, and marry while you can,
 "There's no time to be lost," say I.

When We went out a Fishing!

Last night Tom Snooks, says he to me,
"If you've a mind some fun to see,
I'll take you out with two or three,
 Who mean to go a fishing.
So get a rod, a can and bait,
We start from town precise at eight;
Then, mind, friend Muggs, you're not too late
 To go with us a fishing."

Says I, " I will," so up I goes
To Mr. Spout with my best clothes,
And borrowed what you may suppose,
    To rig me out for fishing.

CHORUS.

With rods and lines, and bait a store,
Enough for half-a-dozen more,
I never shall forget the bore
    Of going out a fishing.

Then off we trudged, thro' dust and sun,
The perspiration off me run;
Thinks I, " I hope this is'nt the fun
    Of going out a fishing."
At length we reached the river side,
And soon upon the glittering tide
Our floats, like little boats did ride
    As floats do when your fishing.
I felt a tug—I tugged again,
And pulled away with might and main,
When up I brought a dog and chain,
    When we were out a fishing.

                    With rods and lines, &c.

Lord, how they laughed to see the prize,
When Snooks (you know is such a size)
Soused in the stream, to our surprise,
    As though to spoil our fishing.
You've heard about " too many cooks,"
And, as we strove to land old Snooks,
We stuck him full of little hooks
    With which we had been fishing.
At length our friend on shore we brought,
He puff'd and blow'd, you'd have thought
A full grown porpoise we had caught,
    When we were out a fishing.

                    With rods and lines, &c.

We brandy'd Snooks—he soon was well,
We plied away, and must I tell
What next to Jimmy Higgs befell,
    When we were out a fishing.
The sun was hot. the grass was green,
He sat himself where cows had been,
And such a sight was his nankeen,
    When we were out a fishing.
I warning took, and on a rail
I, like a bird in nursery tale,
What wagged about his little tail,
Perch'd me up for fishing.
                With rods and lines, &c.

But such mischance—the rail was old,
It broke, and down the bank I roll'd,
Look here! I'm sure I caught a cold
    From going out a fishing.
The mud was soft—my legs are thin—
And farther I kept sinking in,
Until I thought 'twould reach my chin,
    When we were out a fishing.
At last, says I, "this will not suit,"
So out I bawls, when Higgs, the brute,
He lugged me out but left my boot
    Where I had been a fishing.
                With rods and lines, &c.

At two o'clock, the hour agreed—
We sat us down, ourselves to feed;
But fortune was unkind indeed,
    When we were out a fishing.
For Crabb to whom the grub did fall,
Forgot the pies, the beef, and all,
And bottled up three quarts of small,
    What stuff for us a fishing!
But thank my stars, all danger past,
I'll make the cupboard rue my fast,
My first exploit shall be my last,
    Of going out a fishing.
                With rods and lines, &c.

Great Names of Antiquity.

Air :—"Think of Your Head in the Morning."

[By Eugene F. Johnston.]

Of late years parents' a fashion have made
  Of giving great names to their children ;
Such as Diogenes, Snooks, Hannibal, Praed,
  And others e'en more bewildering.
But this custom has become almost absurd,
  To prove it, a few names I'll mention,
And though they seem queer, they are true to the
      word,
  And really none of my invention.

Horace, the ancient, in Gotham does dwell,
  And edits a daily paper ;
Demosthenes (snook) is a dealer in wool,
  And Cicero, a black chimney scraper.
Cromwell's a peeler in the gay Broadway squad,
  George Law has New York in a stable ;
Michael Angelo, the German, carries the hod,
  And Cæsar, waits on a table.

Brutus is a butcher in Christopher street,
  Sebastian, a pilot and coaster ;
Homer's a cobbler that measures the feet,
  Anthony, but a bill-poster.
Bacchus was ne'er known any liquor to use—
  He belongs to a temperance society.
Cleopatra (though some think her morals were
      loose),
  Is considered the pink of propriety.

The Conquerer Hannibal, in chains is now bound,
  By his master the famous Van Amburgh ;
Diana was slaughtered at the dog-pound,
  By the quack doctor, Galen, of Hamburgh.
Fernando holds Mozart's great harp in his hand,
  For "Dixie" he sweetly discourses ;

Benjamin's chief of the "policy band,"
  And deals in "gigs" "saddles" and "horses."

Pompey's a Knight of the dish-cloth and pan,
  Israel a Chatham street tailor;
Lafayette is now Mr. Shoddy's coachman,
  Gustavus, is but a nailer.
Hector who lost a leg at Bull Run,
  Has been lately awarded a pension,
Napoleon the preacher, never handled a gun,
  For fighting he makes no pretension.

Ulysses, still conquers as in days of yore,
  He's the granting success of our nation;
Crœsus is ragged, and miserably poor,
  Almost on the verge of starvation.
So I've proven to you there is nought in a name,
  Be it ever so Grecian or Roman,
Call a man what you will, it's all the same,
  For a name I am sure will make no man.

Things Not Generally Known.

Air :—-"Green Grows the Rushes."

[A Popular Comic Song.]

A tailor's goose will never fly,
  Want of money makes us sad;
An apple dumpling's not a pie,
  Crazy folks are always mad.
A contractor's heart is very small,
  The monument is very high;
One that's dumb can never bawl,
  Very seldom asses die.
            CHORUS.
            Right fol lol, &c.

Irish whiskey's very good,
  Macaboy will make you sneeze,
A barber's block is made of wood,
  The moon is not made of green cheese;
Garters keep the stockings up,
  All bakers are not honest men;
When a dog is young he's call'd a pup,
  The rooster's tougher than the hen.
          Right fol lol, &c.

Wooden legs wear out no shoes,
  Christmas comes but once a year;
Without feet we can't have toes,
  Ten cents will buy a pint of beer.
We all shall live until we die,
  Old maids in scandal take delight;
Topers they are often dry,
  Roguery will come to light.
          Right fol lol, &c.

Tailors cabbage all your cloth,
  Shins of beef are very tough;
Hennessey is just like froth,
  Mrs. Caudle's up to snuff.
Jolly tars are fond of fun,
  For Union we will ever shout;
And now good folks my song is done,
  Nobody knows what 'twas all about.

I've Lately Had Some Money.

Air :---" Statty Fair."

Obscurely I had passed my life,
  Was called an ignoramus,
'Till I, like Byron, woke and found
  Myself, one morning, " famous."

All darkly had life's weather been,
  Tho' now 'tis bright and sunny,
And yet this change is not so strange,
  I've lately had some money.

Where'er I went folks ran away,
  As if from burning lava,
They could not be more frightened at
  The poison'd tree of Java.
'Tis not so now, for all, I vow,
  Flock near, like bees round honey,
Oh! magic change of fortune's wand,
  It's 'cause I've got some money!

I used to say some funny things—
  At least I dared to think so;
But dull upon each ear they fell,
  And all away would shrink so.
My mouth I never open now,
  But all I say is funny,
My jokes oft bring hysterics on—
  I've lately got some money!

Unnoticed I might walk, I'm sure,
  From Bull's Head to the Battery,
For not a man would nod to me,
  Or speak a word of flattery.
But now I never venture out
  But every face is sunny,
And all bob their heads like mandarins—
  Because I've got some money.

On any subject I debate,
  If I a sentence started,
'Twas never listened to—and none
  Cared how with pain I smarted.
My slightest whisper now is heard—
  No more am I their dummy,
They cannot act without me now—
  I've lately had some money.

The Doctor.

A new Parody.

Not a cent had he got, not a treasury note,
  And he looked confusedly flurried,
As he bolted away without paying his shot,
  And the landlady after him hurried.

When we saw him again at the dead of night,
  When home from the club returning,
We twigg'd the doctor beneath the light
  Of gas-lamps dimly burning.

All bare and exposed to the mid-night dews,
  Reclined in the gutter we found him;
And he looked like a gentleman taking a snooze,
  With his marshal cloak around him.

The doctor's as drunk as the devil, we said,
  And we managed a shutter to borrow;
We raised him, and sighed at the thought that his
      head,
  Would so dreadfully ache on the morrow.

We bore him home and we put him to bed,
  And we told his wife and daughter,
To give him next day, a couple of red—
  Herrings, with soda water.

Loudly they talked of his money that's gone,
  And his lady began to upbraid him;
But little he reck'd so they let him snore on
  'Neath the counterpane—just as we laid him.

We tuck'd him in, and had hardly done,
  When beneath the window calling,
We heard the rough voice of a son of a gun
  Of a watchman, " one o'clock" bawling.

Slowly and sadly we all walked down
  From his room in the uppermost story,
A rushlight we placed on the cold hearthstone,
And we left him alone in his glory.

The Cove that Sings.
Air :—" The Cove that Spouts."

No doubt a song you've heard,
  How greatly it delights!
It comprises in a word
  The luck of the cove that writes.
Now I've a song so true,
  (My mind to truth it clings,)
And I'm going to tell you,
  The luck of a cove that sings.
                    Tol de rol, &c.

When at singing I made a start,
  Some said my voice was fine;
I tried a serious part,
  But turned to the comic line.
I found out that was best,
  Some fun it always brings;
To the room it gives a zest,
  And it suits the cove that sings.
                    Tol de lol, &c.

To a concert or a rout,
  Each night I'm asked to go;
With my new toggery I go out,
  And cut no little show;
Goes up to the music all right,
  At the women I sheep's eyes flings,
Gets my lush free all the night,
  Because I'm the cove that sings.

If I go to take a room,
  There is no talk or stuff;

About reference they don't fume,
　My word is quite enough.
For the money they don't care a sous,
　The landlady kind looks flings ;
She's proud to have in her house
　A gentleman that sings.

While strolling t'other night,
　I dropt into a house, d'ye see?
The landlord so polite
　Insisted on treating me ;
I called for a glass of port,
　When a full bottle he brings,
[*Spoken.*] " How much to pay, landlord," said I.
　" Nothing of that sort,"
Says he, " You're the cove that sings."

Now my song is at an end,
　My story through I've run ;
And all that I did intend,
　Was to cause a little fun.
If I succeed, that's right,
　There's a pleasure pleasing brings,
And I'll try some other night
　The luck of a cove that sings.

The Wonderful Man.

Air :---" Derry Down."

There was a man tho' its not very common,
And, as people say, he was born of a woman ;
And if that be true, as I have been told,
He was once an infant, but age made him old.

CHORUS.

Down, Down, Derry Down.

His face was the oddest that ever was seen,
His mouth stood across, 'twixt his nose and his chin,

Whenever he spoke, it was then with his voice,
And in talking he always made some sort of noise.
> Down, Derry, &c.

He'd an arm on each side to work when he pleased,
But never worked hard when he lived at his ease;
Two legs he had got to make him complete,
And, what was more odd at each end of his feet.
> Derry Down.

His legs, as folks say, he could move at his will,
And when he was walking he never stood still;
If you were to see him you'd laugh till you'd burst,
For one leg or 'tother would surely be first.   .
> Derry Down, &c.

And, as people say, if you gave him some meat,
Why if he was hungry, he surely would eat;
And when he is dry if you give him the pot,
The liquor most commonly runs down his throat.
> Derry Down, &c.

If this whimsical fellow had a river to cross,
If he could not get over—he'd stay where he was;
He seldom or ever gets off the dry ground,
So great was his luck that he never was drowned.
> Derry Down, &c.

Another misfortune befel this poor yeoman,
For, when he was married, his wife was a woman.
And if you believe me, tho' he he was reviled,
You may truly aver he was never a child.
> Derry Down.

And if it be true, as I have often heard tell,
When he was sick he was not very well;
He gave a large gasp, opened his mouth wide,
By some means or other this poor fellow died.
> Derry Down, &c.

But the reason he died and the cause of his death,
Was, poor soul! for the want of more breath.
And now he is left in the grave for to moulder,
Had he lived a day longer, he'd be a day older.

> Derry Down, &c.

The Wonderful Nose.

Air :—"King and Countryman."

A curious tale I will now disclose,
Concerning a man with a very long nose!
Like an elephant's trunk it reached to his toes,
And with it he could deal out some terrible blows.

CHORUS.

> Ri tu ral lu, &c.

This wonderful nose he could swing left and right,
Which you all must allow looked a comical sight,
No one dare come near him so great was his might,
A blow from his nose would settle 'em quite.

> Ri tu ral, &c.

This terrible chap was about nine feet high,
With a comical squint and a mouth all awry,
Though bandy his legs his heels were so light,
He'd just give a spring and jump out of sight.

> Ri tu ral, &c.

The hair on his head sprouted out like a leek,
And whenever he spoke 'twas a kind of a squeak;
He would oft with his nose, toss up men for a freak,
And never came down, 'tis said, for a week.

> Ri tu ral, &c.

This chap wore a hat in shape like a basin,
With a brim wide enough for a donkey to race on.

And such a deuce of a fellow he was to take snuff,
That a pound at a pinch was hardly enough.
> Ri tu ral, &c.

The country was filled with wonder and dread,
So the king at last set a price on his head;
And so loud did he snore when at night in bed,
'Twas said if he lived, he would soon wake the dead.
> Ri tu ral, &c.

Some guards of the king at last made a gap,
Through the doors of the house of this terrible chap,
They found him in bed just taking a nap,
With his nose round his head in place of his cap.
> Ri tu ral, &c.

They crept one by one tip-toe on the floor,
I think that in all there was near twenty score;
They tried to secure him, but mark what a bore,
He jump'd through the roof and was never seen
> more.
> Ri tu ral, &c.

The soldiers were all of them struck with afright,
When they saw Mr. Nosey cut clean out of sight,
And so angry were they he had taken his flight,
They set to and punched each other all night.
> Ri tu ral, &c.

Grumbling People.

Air :—" Good Morrow to your Nightcap."

It's wonderful in this bright world,
    Where all our wants supplied are,
And freedom's flag is never furled,
    Folks so dissatisfied are;

Tho fortune yields her gifts to those
  Who, station once were humble in,
To peace of mind they still are foes,
  And ever will keep grumbling!

CHORUS.

So this indeed is true, you'll find,
  Whatever life you tumble in;
Both high and low, nay, all mankind,
  They always will be grumbling!

There's Mr. Snoggins and his wife,
  They lead a life bewildering;
Forever they were both at strife
  Because they had no children;
The other day she brought him three,
  (A tidy batch to tumble in,)
One would have thought that pleased he'd be,
  Yet still he keeps on grumbling!

Then there's the milliner, Miss Wren,
  So crabb'd and sour in features,
She vows she can't bear the men,
  The nasty, frightful creatures!
Her age is forty-three—no less,
  Her pride there is no humbling,
She's left to single-blessedness,—
  Yet still she keeps on grumbling!

The Doctor grumbles (truth to tell,)
  'Cause people are too healthy;
While they keep obstinately well,
  He never can grow wealthy;
He says, "its very hard, he's sure,"
  His vanity it's humbling,—
But had he half mankind to cure,
  He still would keep on grumbling!

The undertaker grave does look,
  His feelings he can't master,
He thinks by fortune he's forsook

'Cause people don't die faster !
If in their graves, (the greedy elf,)
  All New York had to tumble in,—
And the job to bury 'em all himself,
  The fellow would keep grumbling !

The topers have a bitter pill—
  (In their bowels feel it rumbling ;)
For, physic'd by the late tax-bill,
  They'll never cease their grumbling !
In short, it needs no pains to show,
  Or any further mumbling,
That old and young, both high and low,
  Throughout the world are grumbling !

The Steam Cigar.
Air :—" Cork Leg."

A song I'll sing, a regular joker,
Of a man, a terrible smoker ;
He smoked away from night till morn,
'Tis said, he smoked when he was born.

CHORUS.

        Ri tu ral,&c.

He tried Havanna, Cuba, too,
He tried tobacco, none would do,
To please him none of them did seem,
So he had a cigar to smoke by steam.

        Ri tu ral, &c.

He lit his cigar, and he puff'd the smoke,
With such force that it a window broke ;
And then the heat it was so strong,
He burnt the folks as he walked along.

        Ri tu ral, &c.

It burnt away to his heart's desire,
Some people thought the city on fire ;
And if he went out when it chanced to rain,
His lighted cigar dried it up again.

> Ri tu ral, &c.

When into a room his nose he pokes,
They all cry out " the chimney smokes!"
And then his cigar makes such a smell,
That people declare it's just like —— !"

> Ri tu ral, &c.

'Tis said in London,—and this is no joke,
" 'Tis him that makes us in such a smoke,"
When of a night he's seen afar,
He's taken by all for the evening star.

> Ri tu ral, &c.

One day when on a mountain top
Folks thought him a comet, ready to drop,
And some saw from afar the sight,
And thought it was the sun's gas light.

> Ri tu ral, &c.

He smoked away to his heart's desire,
Till death appeared and quenched the fire.
He put out his cigar for a bit of a lark,
And then at once extinguished the spark.

> Ri tu ral, &c,

The Chapter of Accidents.

Air :—"Bow Wow."

I'll tell you of sad accidents a long and dismal
     chapter,
For if bad luck had e'er a form, they to my back
     have strapped her;
I never once a wooing went in all my useful life,
     sir,
Or ten to one, but I had got Miss Fortune for a
     wife, sir.

When I was young, as I've heard say, they never
     used the ladle,
Without they burnt my infant throat, or else
     upset the cradle;
Once when a boy, on going to school, as gay as any
     fairy,
While looking up at a large crow, I tumbled down
     an area.

One day, at play, my teacher cried, mind what
     you're with that ball about;
So taking care to strike it low, I knocked my
     master's eye-ball out;
And being frightened, tried to find my way out by
     a shorter cut,
By running down a flight of stairs I fell into a
     water butt.

Without misfortune one whole day, I thought
     good luck complying;
I went to bed so light of heart, I dreampt that I was
     flying;
Then up I got, resolved to sing, with angels fair, a
     song on high,
Threw up the window, out I jumped into a mud
     cart passing by.

Beneath a scaffold walking once, with Dobbins and
    his daughter,
In looking up, plump on my head came down a
    hod of mortar;
A voice above cried "mind below" so I tried to run
    to tell her,
But flurried push'd her in the mud, her father
    down a cellar.

Challenged once to fight, but shedding blood, in
    fear of,
I turned about to waste my fire, but shot my
    second's ear off;
Returning home, a porter met, with heavy load of
    brass work,
I slipp'd my foot, and shoved him through, a
    window full of glass work.

Once at an inn, not liking fuss, I to my room was
    creeping
But there mistook the chamber door, and found a
    lady sleeping;
And running out her husband met, in state of fierce
    distraction
Who bang'd me well about the head, then brought
    a crim-con action.

Once at a ball my foot gave way, when I thought
    to grace a jig
I falling tripp'd my partner up,—pull'd off an old
    lady's wig;
Then, sore abashed, I left the room, quite blinded
    by my bitter cares,
And slipping off the landing place, shoved three
    young ladies down the stairs.

Some thieves one night the parlor robbed, but they
    could get no higher,
Watched next night, fell fast asleep, and set the
    house on fire;

More accidents I would recount, in hopes that you
    might note them,
But by mistake I've thrown away the book in
    which I've wrote them.

The Twig of the Shannon.

On the beautiful banks of the Shannon,
   There grows such an illigant tree,
And the first that it bears is shilalah,
   I've a sprig of it here you may see.
'Tis the remnant of all my large fortune,
   It's my friend that ne'er play'd me a trick,
And I'd rather loose half my supportin'
   Than part with this illigant stick.

CHORUS.

'Twas a delicate sprig in the summer,
   When I first cut it from the tree,
And I've kept it through all the cold weather,
   Faix the sprig of shilalah for me.

It's the porter that carried my luggage,
   For I've shouldered it many a mile,
And from thieves it will safely protect me,
   In a beautiful, delicate style.
Its useful for rows in the summer,
   And when winter comes on with a storm,
If you're short of a fire in the cabin,
   You can burn it to keep yourself warm.
               'Twas a delicate, &c.

Its a friend both so true and so constant,
   It's constancy pen cannot paint;
For it always is there when it's wanted,
   And sometimes its there when it aint;

It beats all your guns and your rifles,
  For it goes off whene'er you desire,
And it's sure to hit what'er it's aimed at,
  For shillalah's they never miss fire.
                  'Twas &c.

It's a talisman so upright and honest,
  Twenty shillings it pays to the pound ;
So if ever it gets you in debt, sir,
  You are sure to be paid I'll be bound.
It never runs up a long score, sir,
  In trade it's not given to fail,
There's no danger of it's being insolvent,
  For it always pays down on the nail.
                 'Twas &c.

And faith at an Irish election,
  An argument striking it's there ;
For with brickbats and sprigs of the Shannon
  We see things go all right and square,
It's then there's no bribery at all, sir,
  They vote as they like, every soul,
But it's no use opposing shilalah,
  Or it's sure to come down on the poll.
                 'Twas &c.

The Wants of the People.

Air :—" When the Saxon."

As you want a song I could sing for a moon,
But it happens I want both a subject and tune ;
You want and I want suppose I e'en bawl,
About wants entirely of great folks and small ;

CHORUS.

For barring all pother, of this want and t'other,
We all of us want in our turn.

The infant wants gewgaws and rattles so gay,
The child wants with others to go out and play;
The youth wants to leave school and learning so
flat,
Whimsical folks want—they never know what.
> For barring all pother, &c.

The man wants a wife, which want sticks in his
head,
Till he weds her, he then wants another instead;
The sick man wants health and takes bolus and
pill,
The doctor wants—only to make a long bill:
> For barring all pother, &c.

The lawyer wants clients, and drains them with
glee,
The physician a visit pays—then wants his fee;
The tailor wants custom and for it he looks,
His customers all want to get in his books;
> For barring all pother, &c.

The Sailor wants grog and tobacco galore,
His money spent then wants to sail out for more,
The soldier wants ease after battle and strife,
The prisoner wants liberty—sweet balm of life.
> For barring all pother, &c.

The clerk to be master, wants to aspire,
His master from business wants to retire,
Fancies his cash makes a gentleman true,
Takes a villa, and then—he wants something to do.
> For barring all pother, &c

Some great politicians, with feeling so warm,
Want to persuade us we want to reform;
They get into office, and then plainly we trace,
Like many more members they want a good
place.
> For barring all pother, &c.

So numerous our wants, they with each other vie,
Poor folks all want rich relations to die;
Our wants for the most part are futile and vain.
Many folks want what they never obtain;
>> For barring all pother, &c.

The apple wants limbs, the fool he wants sense,
The nation wants millions for its defence;
They just now want a little less tax,
And shoddy contractors, want only contracts.
>> For barring all pother, &c.

Thus all mankind want, but for fear you should
>> scoff,
I'll end, for perhaps you want me to leave off;
So about that or this want at present I'll pause,
I've only one want now,—and that your applause;
>> For barring all pother, &c.

Alteration and Improvement.
Air :—" Bow Wow."

Oh, when I was a little boy, I noticed every move-
>> ment,
And little thought so short a time, would bring so
>> much improvement;
Now the world is turning upside down in observa-
>> tion,
For, turn which way you will, you'll find there's
>> naught but alteration.

Before the march of intellect, the ladies, e'en the
>> oddest,
Dress'd themselves all neat and prim, and look'd so
>> very modest,
Now by many habits they are led in imitation,
For all wear trowsers, and, of course, that makes
>> an alteration.

Before the march of intellect, (indeed I am not
    joking),
Our grandfathers and fathers would indulge them-
    selves in smoking;
Now the vulgar pipes of clay are banished from the
    nation,
And everybody smokes cigars, and that's an alter-
    ation.

Before the march of intellect, our servant maids all
    dress'd in
Neat check aprons, and what hats their mistress-
    es thought best in ;
Now girls despise all check and apron, too, in
    every station,
And gents' now wear check trav'ling shirts, and
    that's an alteration.

Before the march of intellect, folks never thought
    of trials,
For throwing light additional on watches, clocks,
    or dials ;
Now old time is lit with gas, with clocks illumina-
    tion,
And citizens enlightened are—and that's an altera-
    tion.

Before the march of intellect, our soldiers all wore
    big tails,
Beaux would strut in clean shorn faces, powder'd
    heads and pig tails;
Dandies now by whiskers big are led in imitation,
And monkeys wear mustachios, and that's an alter-
    ation.

Thus whilst we see so many changes floating all
    around,
May the march of intellect in every walk abound;
May fashion and variety be seen all o'er the nation,
And may we find improvement good in every al-
    teration.

Never Cut Your Toe Nails On a Sunday.

[A Popular Comic Song.]

A dashing young fellow, one Mr. John Lowe,
  Walked fifth Avenue on a fine Sunday;
His dress was the pink of the fashion and go,
  When he met with the charming Miss Gundy;
Her beautiful eyes took him quite by surprise,
  And so queer was the state that he felt in;
He tried all in vain to tell his pain
  For his heart it was really a melting.

CHORUS.

But, alas, who can look into fate's book of laws,
  Mr. Lowe would have married Miss Gundy;
He lost her! he lost her!—and only because,—
  He cut his toe-nails on a Sunday.

The next time he met her his love he made known,
  Her person he thought all perfection,
He press'd her with speed to be bone of his bone,
  She blush'd, and—had no objection.
He gaily did sing, went and purchased the ring,
  And the next Sunday was the bespeak day,
For that day would chime, and agree with his time,
  Much better than having a week day.

  But, alas!

On the blest Sunday morning he got up with glee,
  (Little thinking that mischief was hatching,)
Took out his pen knife for his toes to make free,
  At night to prevent them from scratching.
But the knife slipt and gave his big toe a wound;
  (Sweet wedlock there's surely a fate in)
That he could'nt put it at all on the ground,
  Tho' he knew Miss Gundy was waiting.

  But, alas!

Oh! words can't describe all his trouble and woe,
   Only think of his sad destination;
A surgeon was sent for, who dressed his big toe,
   And talked all about amputation!
Laid up for a month, while Miss Gundy so smart,
   Disappointed of having this short knight,
Without delay got her another sweetheart,
   And married in less than a fortnight!

So young men, if love has got into your head,
   Recollect Mr. Lowe and Miss Gundy;
And whatever you do before you get wed,
   Never cut your toe nails on a Sunday.

The Removal.

Air :—"Derry Down."

A nervous old gentleman tired of trade—
By which, though it seems, he a fortune had made,
Took a house! 'twixt two sheds at the skirts of the
   town,
Which he meant, at his leisure, to buy and pull
   down.
            CHORUS.
              Down, Down, &c.

This thought struck his mind when he view'd the
   estate,
But alas! when he entered he found it too late;
For in each dwelt a smith—a more hard working
   two
Never doctored a patient, or put on a shoe.
              Down, Down, &c.

At six in the morning, their anvils at work,
Awoke our good squire who swore like a Turk;
"These fellows" he cried, " such a clattering keep,
That I never can get above eight hours sleep."
              Down, Down, &c.

From morning till night, they kept thumping
 away,—
No sound but the anvil the whole of the day;
His afternoon's nap, and his daughter's new song,
Were banished and spoiled by the hammers' ding
 dong.

    Down, Down, &c.

He offered each Vulcan to purchase his shop,
But no! they were stubborn, determined to stop;
At length (both his spirits and health to improve,)
He cried, "I'll give each fifty dollars to move."

    Down, Down, &c.

"Agreed!" said the pair, "that will make us
 amends."
"Then come to my house, and let us part friends;
You shall dine; and we'll drink on this joyous
 occasion,
That each may live long in his new habitation."

    Down, Down, &c.

He gave the two blacksmiths a sumptuous regale—
He spared not provisions, his wine or his ale;
So much was he pleased with the thought that each
 guest
Would take from him noise and restore him to rest.

    Down, Down, &c.

"And now" said he, "tell me, where mean you to
 move—
I hope to some spot where your trade may improve?"
"Why, sir," replied one, with a grin on his phiz,
"Tom Forge moves to my shop and I—move to
 his."

    Down, Down, &c.

He was only One of the Rank and File.

'Twas a glorious day worth a warrior's telling,
  Two kings had fought and the fight was done,
When amidst the shouts of victory swelling,
  A soldier fell on the field he had won.
He thought of kings and of royal quarrels ;
  He thought of glory, without a smile,
For, what had he to do with laurels
  He was only one of the rank and file.

CHORUS.

  Then, taking his little cruiskeen !
    He drank to his pretty colleen,
  Oh ! darling, said he, if I die,
    You won't be a widow, for why ?
  Sure, you would never have me, vourneen !

A raven tress from his bosom taking
  That now was stained with his life stream shed ;
And a fervent prayer on that ringlet making,
  He blessings sought for that loved one's head ;
And visions fair of his native mountains,
  Arose enchanting his fading sight
Her emerald valleys and chrystal fountains,
  Were never shining more clear and bright.

  Then taking his little cruiskeen,
    He pledged his dear island so green,
  Tho' far from thy vallies I die !
    Dearest isle of my heart, thou art nigh !—
  As though absent I never had been.

A tear now fell for his life was sinking,
  The pride that guarded that manly eye
Had weaker grown, such tender thinking,
  Brought home, and Heaven, and his true-love
      nigh.
But with the fire of his gallant nation !
  He scorned surrender without a blow ;

He met with death's capitulation,
  And with warlike honors he still would go.
    Then draining his little cruiskeen,
    He drank to his cruel colleen,
  To the emerald land of his birth,
    Then lifeless, he sank to the earth,
  Brave a soldier as ever was seen.

Paddy from Cork.

[As sung by Billy O'Neil, J. H. Ogden, &c.]

Dublin's a duck of a city,
  'Tis built as you go to Ratfarnham,
Limerick gloves are so pretty,
  That Limerick lasses they darn 'em ;
At Belfast they sell ready made pork,
  If they meet with a mad bull they don't
      mind him,
I there met Paddy from Cork,
  Who buttoned his coat behind him.
          CHORUS.
             Tu ral, lu, &c.

Irishmen all love the sod,
  Whiskey will bother the tooth-ache ;
And love, tho' it sounds mighty odd,
  Make the hearts of the boys in truth ache ;
Shelah's mother cried " girl never talk,
  Of that ugly paudeen never mind him,
There's mischief in Paddy from Cork,
  When he buttons his coat behind him !"
             Tu ral lu, &c.

Now Paddy of good looks did'nt lack,
  And his tongue it was tipp'd with blarney,
Yet he had'nt a brogue to his back,
  (Except two on his feet) from Killarney.

Upper leather of wood did'nt baulk
　　His steps, when a jig inclined him,—
Like a divil danced Paddy from Cork,
　　When his coat it was buttoned behind him.
　　　　　　　　Tu ral lu, &c.

At Ballanashlinch on fair days,
　　When he threw down his modest shillalah,
Divils cure to one, that said—Peace
　　He got Eringobra gallant gaily;
For hay, or beefsteak, he'd a fork,
　　Work or meat to no limit confined him,
Such a vourneen was Paddy from Cork,
　　When his coat it was buttoned behind him.
　　　　　　　　Tu ral lu, &c.

Mr. and Mrs. Skinner.

　" I really think it very kind,
　　This visit, Mrs. Skinner,
　I have not seen you in such an age—
[*Aside*]—The wretch has come to dinner!

　"Your daughters too!—what loves of girls,
　　What heads for painter's easels,
　Come here, and kiss the infant, dears;—
[*Aside*]—And give it, p'raps the measles!

　" Your charming boys I see are home,
　　From Reverend Mr. Russel's,
　'Twas very kind to bring them both!—
[*Aside.*]—What boots for my new brussels!

　"So Mr. S. I hope he's well,
　　And, though he lives so handy,
　He never now drops in to sup;
[*Aside.*]—The better for our brandy!

" Come take a seat I long to hear
    About Matilda's marriage ;
You've come of course to spend the day,—
Aside.]—Thank Heavens, I hear the carriage !

" What! must you go—next time, I hope
    You'll give me longer measure,
Nay, I shall see you down the stairs,
[*Aside.*]—With most uncommon pleasure !

"Good bye! good bye! remember all,
    Next time you take your dinners :
Now, John, mind, I'm ' not at home,'
    In future to the Skinners."

Parody on " Mother, I've Come Home to Die."

(An Original Conglomeration of titles, by the popular Author Eugene T. Johnston.)

Dear Mother, I remember well
    " That nice young gal from New Jersey,"
She said, " Oh kiss but never tell !"
    " How are you, black horse cavalry ?"
"Then let me like a soldier fall,"
    " When the swallows homeward fly ;"
" Come landlord fill the flowing bowl"
    " Dear Mother, I've come home to die."

CHORUS.

" Call me pet names" " Annie Lisle,"
    " A bully boy with a glass eye ;"
" Oh let her rip she's all O. K,"
    " Dear Mother, I've come home to die."

" Oh, hark ! I hear an angel sing,"
    " I'll be free and easy still,"
" My love he is a sailor boy,"
    With "The sword of Bunker Hill."

Oh "Happy happy be thy dreams,"
  When you're "Coming thro' the rye;"
"I wish I was in Dixie's land"
  "Dear Mother, I've come home to die."
          " Call me pet names, &c.

" Dear Tom," "'Twas my grand-ma's advice"
  " Don't ever fly your kite too high;"
"I'm over young to marry yet"
  "Says the spider to the fly."
" We met by chance" at "Donnybrook fair"
  Where " No Irish need apply;"
" I dream't I dwelt in marble halls"
  "Dear Mother, I've come home to die."
          " Call me pet names," &c.

" Yes dearest I will love thee more,"
  " I'll hang my harp on a willow tree,"
" Our Billy was a butcher boy,"
  And "Sally is the gal for me."
" A dainty plant's the ivy green,"
  " Then comrades raise your banners high;"
" I wish I had a fat contract,"
  "Dear Mother, I've come home to die."
          " Call me pet names," &c.

Barney Brallaghan.

'Twas on a windy night, about two o'clock in the
          morning,
An Irish lad so tight, all wind and weather scorn-
          ing ;
At Judy Callaghan's door, sitting upon the pailing,
His love tale he did pour, and this is part of his
          wailing,

CHORUS.

Only say—you'll be Mistress Brallaghan,
Don't say nay—charming Judy Callaghan.

Oh! list to what I say, charms you've got like
    Venus,
Own your love you may, for there's only the wall
    between us.
You lay fast asleep, snug in bed and snoring,
While round the house I creep—your hard heart
    imploring.

           Then do say, &c.

I've got an acre of ground, I've got it set with
    praties,
I've got tobacco a pound, and I've got some tea for
    the ladies,
I've got a ring to wed, some whiskey, to make us
    gaily,
A mattress feather bed and a handsome new
    shillaly.

           Then do say, &c.

I've got an old tom cat, which though one eye is
    staring
I've got a Sunday hat, a little the worse for wear-
    ing,
A Sunday hose and coat, and old gray mare to ride
    on,
A saddle and bridle to boot, that you may ride as-
    tride on.

           If you'll say, &c.

I've got nine pigs and a sow, and I've got a sty to
    keep 'em,
A calf and a brindle cow, and I've a cabin to sleep
    'em,
I've got some gooseberry wine, the trees they grew
    no riper on.

           When you say, &c.

You've got a charming eye, you've got some spell-
    ing and reading,

You've got, and so have I, a taste for genteel
          breeding;
You're rich and fair and young, as everybody's
          knowing,
And you've got a decent tongue whenever you set
          it a going.

> Then do say, &c.

Oh! for a wife till death, I am willing to take you,
But oh! I spend my breath, the devil himself can't
          wake you,
'Tis just beginning to rain—so I'll get under cover,
I'll come to-morrow again to be your constant lover.

> If you'll say, &c.

Ireland, the Land of Shilalah Law.

Air :—Paddy O'Carroll.

Och! Ireland the place is, for Grecians and graces,
  For sweetest of faces the world ever saw ;
For fighting genteely and drinking too freely,
  Potatoes so mealy, and sweet usquebaugh.
Och! the paddies are rare ones, the ladies are fair,
      ones,
  And no one there dare once to say they are not;
If Barney were by now, his cudgel would ply now,
  And make him soon fly now, as quick as a shot.

CHORUS.

For he's of the nation of civilization,
  Of sweet botheration and shillalah law ;
Och! a good tough skull-breaker's the best of all
      speakers,
  Sing filliloo! hubbubboo! Erin go braugh !

Sweet Judy O'Connor, a maid of true honor,
  So neatly I won her at Donnybrook Fair,

From Paddy M'Fingal, an Ulsterman single,
  Who came in a jinjle, and sported her there.
Och! Judy, I cried now, how can you ride now,
  And have at your side now, such a bandy-legged
      knave?
Och! cried Paddy, Barney, pray give us no blarney,
  Or faith! I'll soon learn ye now how to behave.

     To the sprig of the nation, &c.

Pat's cudgel was handy, and though he was bandy,
  He was quite the dandy in love or a fight;
He gave me a topper—I gave him a whopper,
  It was such a stopper it stopped his mouth quite;
His courage was all out, he murder did bawl out,
  " And why did we fall out, sweet Barney, my
      joy?''
Och! if you'd know why, now, for Judy I'd die
    now,
  Take that in your eye, now, dear Paddy my boy.

     For I'm of the nation, &c.

So Judy, I caught her, but very soon after,
  She did die a martyr to whisky so strong;
There was a grand making at sweet Judy's waking,
  Lights, whisky, and cake, in galore the night
    long;
As Judy did lie now, her friends all did cry now—
  Och! why did you die now, and leave us to-
    nignt?
Till with liquor o'ertaken, we got to heads break-
    ing,
  And finished the wake in—a row and a fight.

     For we're of the nation, &c.

Long Barney.

Air :—" Kate Kearney."

Did you ever hear tell of Long Barney ?
He dwelt near the groves of Killarney ;
One glance from his eye caused the girls all to sigh,
For they had a liking for Barney.

I'll sing to you now of his fightin',
A thing which he took great delight in ;
He could handle the sthick, all the boys he could
         lick,
And they all stood in fear of Long Barney. -

He went to the fair—it was Aisther ;
In his pocket had many the tasther ;
He met Biddy Briggs, and wid her had jigs,
And she fell deep in love wid Long Barney.

So into a tent he did take her,
And he called for a drop of the crather ;
Wid his arms round her waist, her sweet lips he
         did taste,
"Oh!" she cried, " don't you smother me, Barney ?"

So up steps one Darby O'Brien,
And Biddy, he long had his eye on ;
"Arrah, Biddy," says he, " come over till me,
An' don't stop there whisperin' till Barney."

Says Barney, " I'll soon make him toddle,
If I hit him a pelt on the noddle ; "
Arrah, whack! goes the stick, on the floor Darby
         kicks;
" Faith, I've dusted his jacket," says Barney.

So Barney sits down by his Biddy,
For the whisky and fight made him giddy ;

" If there's arah spalpeen 'ill step out on the green,
Faith, I'll scuttle his noddle," says Barney.

Wid a great deal of coaxin' an' twistin',
Says Biddy, " There's no resistin';
There's my father, Tim Briggs, says he's give a pig
To the man that'll marry me, Barney."

So now they're united together,
And they stick till each other like leather;
There's Barney and Briggs, little children and pigs,
And they all sleep together with Barney.

The Airy Flower.

Air :—"The Prairie Flower."

Down the kitchen airy, when the mutton smil'd,
In its luscious beauty, roast or b'ild,
Crept a knowing Bobby, who possess'd the power
Of knowing Betty's dinner hour,
In her cozy kitchen, not a little wild,
Once she kept the supper 'till 'twas sp'ild,
And the gravy dried up, so (the case was rare)
She felt somewhat inclined to swear.

CHORUS.

" Where is my Bobby?   Where can he be?
To-night he was to come and sup with me!
I've had a Hirish stew a-ready for this hour,
For Bobby Lee, the Airy Flower!"

Oh! the case was rare, he never stayed so long,
From his little fairy—thought it wrong
To keep a lady waiting, and what's even worse,
The dish he loved so well, of course.
When the twilight shadows gather'd in the west,
And the voice of hunger wouldn't let him rest,

Like a crushing feeling not a little ril'd,
Lest Betty's temper should be sp'ild.

"There is my lilly," softly sang he,
" The light's in the airy, waiting for me.
Every one who knows her feels her gentle
power,
Like Bobby Lee, the Airy Flower."

Feeling somewhat jaded, Betty upward cast,
A look—exclaiming, " Here he comes at last !
Oh ! he oughter been here (leavin' me forlorn)
Mor'n two long hours agone !"

Scarce had these angels whisper'd in each ear,
When lo! " What's that—a footstep ? 'tis, I fear !"
Cried Bobby, and he swore a wicked oath that
night,
Then cunningly put out the light.

Down came the missis, close to the door,
Bob made for the airy, Betty scream'd ' Oh, lor !
I thought 'twas Barnum's ghost, mum, a tak-
ing off his tow'r,
Like Bobby Lee, the Airy Flower !"

Poor Old Horse Let Him Die.

My clothing once, alas my friends, was linsey wool-
sey fine,
My hair was brush'd off neatly, and gaily it did
shine ;
But now I am a growing old, and nature doth de-
cay,
My master he doth frown on me, and thus I heard
him say :

CHORUS.
You're good for nothing now Old Horse !
And then he passed me by,
I cannot give you Hay and Oats !
Poor Old Horse let him die.

My lodging once was on clean straw, and in a stable
      warm,
To keep my active sturdy limbs from taking cold
      or harm,
But now I am in open fields, compell'd in truth to
      go,
And bear cold frosty winters, the rain, the hail and
      snow.

                 You're good for, &c.

My feed was once the best of oats, and likewise well
      cur'd hay,
As ever grew upon the lawn, or in the meadows
      gay;
But no such comfort now I find, in the stable or
      clean stall,
I am forc'd to nab the short grass, that grows
      around the wall.

                 You're good for, &c.

My shoulders were both fat and fine, and clean and
      smooth and round,
But corrupted, rotten and my wind it is unsound;
And my founder'd old crack'd hoof, that once was
      smooth and hard,
Is deem'd to be unworthy, to tread my master's
      yard.

                 You're good for, &c.

You eat my hay that's costly, you also spoil my
      straw,
You're not fit to ride, old horse, and my cart you
      cannot draw;
And you are blind and lame old horse, you're lazy,
      dull and slow,
I'll drive you from my premises, to hunt your liv-
      ing go.

                 You're good for, &c.

My skin unto the Huntsman the tale who can be-
    lieve?
My flesh unto the hungry hounds, I shortly too
    must give,
And noble form once nimble, that travell'd leagues
    and miles,
O'er mountains, hedges, ditches, and leap'd o'er
    gates and stiles.
                 You're good for, &c.

The Shoddy Contractor.

Air :—Fine "Old Irish Gentleman."—By E. T. Johnson.

I'll sing to you a little song, made by a modern pate,
About a shoddy cloth-contractor, who owns a fine
    estate:
In a street called Fifth avenue, where big bugs
    congregate,
And bears a good character though his hours are
    somewhat late,
    This shoddy cloth contractor of the present time.

Before this "cruel war" broke out, he was what's
    termed a "beat,"
And kept a small hand-me-down store in Chatham
    street;
His neighbors they all marked him down, as an
    arrant cheat,
But now he'll pass his poor friend by when'er they
    chance to meet,
    This shoddy cloth contractor, one of the present
    time.

Now he keeps a stud of horses, the fastest in the
    town,
Determined to outshine his neighbors Smith and
    Brown;

In Broadway you may see him daily driving up
    and down,
And often at Delmonico's sipping champagne he is
    found,
  This shoddy cloth contractor, one of the present
    time.

He keeps his shoddy factory in a bye street near
    Broadway,
Employs several hundred hands but gives them
    little pay;
And if a poor soldier's wife works hard, she can
    earn fifty cents a day,
To support her little ones at home, while her hus-
    band's far away,
  From this shoddy cloth contractor, one of the
    present day.

At the Sanitary fair, his name is on the list,
Of subscribers for one hundred dollars, but of course
    that won't be missed;
He rents the finest pew in church and always stands
    the grist,
For the next government contract puts fifty thou-
    sand in the fist,
  Of this shoddy cloth contractor, one of the pres-
    ent time.

At every war meeting, he is sure to be seen there,
On the speaker's platform, sometimes he takes the
    chair;
Tho' he can no more make a speech than Barnum's
    grizzly bear,
But he pays a man to write one, which he studies
    with great care.
  This shoddy cloth contractor, one of the present
    time.

You can tell him in a thousand by his lofty mien
    and tread,

This shoddy cloth contractor, who has his country
    bled ;
But tho' justice may be sleeping, still she is not
    dead,
And soon will her avenging sword fall upon the
    heads—
Of all shoddy contractors, of the present time.

All Mankind Are Worms.

Air :—" Bow, wow, wow."

As all us mortals turn to clay,
    When closed our mortal terms, sir,
I think we may, with reason say,
    That all mankind are *worms*, sir.
But as there's some may doubt this truth,
    And I like to be exact, sir,
Your patience kindly grant me, while
    I'll try to prove the fact, sir.

CHORUS.
              Bow, wow, wow.

The Dandy he's a *tape*-worm,
    Made up of stays and lace, sir,
The Tailor he's a *cabbage*-worm,
    That cuts your leaves with grace, sir.
The Lover he's a *glow*-worm,
    That shines but to allure, sir,
The Husband he's a *ring*-worm,
    That old wives best can cure, sir.

              Bow, wow, wow.

The Glutton he's a *meal*-worm,
    Still feeding night and day, sir.
The Drunkard, he's a *still*-worm,
    That drinks his all away, sir.

The Brewer he's a *malt*-worm,
   A very jolly one, sir,
The Farmer he's a *grub*-worm,
   That grubs on in the sun, sir.
               Bow, wow, wow.

The Scholar he's a *book*-worm.
   That best on learning feeds, sir,
The Miser he's a *muck*-worm,
   That on a dunghill breeds, sir.
The Rogue he's but a *blind*-worm,
   That works on in the dark, sir,
The Coquette she's a *bait*-worm,
   That angles for a spark, sir.
               Bow, wow, wow.

The Idler he's a *slow*-worm,
   With laziness he's rife, sir,
The Soldier he's a *blood*-worm,
   Still feeding upon life, sir.
A Maid she is a *silk*-worm,
   That changes every day, sir,
And Love '*a worm in bud*' is,
   That eats our peace away, sir.
               Bow, wow, wow.

And thus, I think I've prov'd to you,
   That all mankind are worms, sir,
Of different kinds and natures, too,
   And different shapes and forms, sir.
And since that all our bodies go
   To the worms at our tail end, sir,
Let's hope, like jolly *butterflies*,
   That we may all ascend, sir.
               Bow, wow, wow.

The Reason Why She Left Him.

Answer to " Why Did She Leave Him ?"

Why did she leave him ?—Oh dear ! what a bother,
And fuss they are making everywhere !
The reason I'll tell you : why she had another,
And to call her deceitful is hardly fair.
He would stop out all night with girls of the fashion,
And would leave her in sorrow, which, you know, is
      a sin ;
He would drink like a fish, had a terrible passion ;
That's one of the reasons why she has left him.

They say : he is united ; but that is a blunder.
In a drunken frolic, make no mistake, he is all there,
He would halloo and bawl, and roar like the thunder,
And quarrel with all when he went to the fair.
He was jealous, and vain, and very conceited,
And if got married, she knows what would begin :
A pair of black eyes would be often repeated,
And this is the reason why she has left him.

She has married another, and he keeps a carriage,
At least so the poets, who wrote of her say :
It's a donkey and cart,—I've no wish to disparage,
Her pride's only seen when she goes to the play ;
But if she walks out in the evening hours,
And sees her old bore, when drinking gin,
She quick hastens home, thanks her stars by the
      powers,
And she is now very glad she has left him.

THE END.